P9-BBV-776
TITANIA
OBERON
PUCK
BOTTOM

WILLIAM SHAKESPEARE'S

A MIDSUMMER NIGHT'S DREAM

RETOLD BY BRUCE COVILLE

PICTURES BY DENNIS NOLAN

Dial Books NEW YORK

For Puck

B. C. & D. N.

Published by Dial Books
A Division of Penguin Books USA Inc.
375 Hudson Street
New York, New York 10014

Typography by Jane Byers Bierhorst
Printed in the U.S.A.
First Edition
1 3 5 7 9 10 8 6 4 2

Library of Congress Cataloging in Publication Data

Coville, Bruce.
William Shakespeare's A midsummer night's dream
retold by Bruce Coville ; pictures by Dennis Nolan.—1st ed.
p. cm.
Summary: A simplified prose retelling of Shakespeare's play about
the strange events that take place in a forest inhabited by fairies who
magically transform the romantic fate of two young couples.
ISBN 0-8037-1784-9.—ISBN 0-8037-1785-7 (lib. bdg.)
[1. Shakespeare, William, 1564–1616—Adaptations.]
I. Shakespeare, William, 1564–1616. Midsummer night's dream.
II. Nolan, Dennis, ill. III. Title.
PR2878.M6C68 1996 822.3'3—dc20 94-12600 CIP AC

The artwork was prepared with graphite
and watercolor on watercolor paper.

Once in ancient Athens a dark-haired girl named Hermia loved a dreamy poet called Lysander. He loved her as well and the couple had promised to marry. But Hermia's father had other ideas.

"It is my right to choose your husband," he told his daughter, "and I choose Demetrius. He's every bit as noble as your Lysander, and he doesn't have his head in the clouds."

"But Father," Hermia protested, "I do not love Demetrius. And further, he is changeable as midsummer weather."

Indeed Hermia spoke the truth. Not long before, Demetrius had pledged his love to Hermia's best friend, Helena. Now he had cast Helena aside to ask for Hermia's hand in marriage.

Still, Hermia's father would not be swayed. "You will marry Demetrius or lose your life." Sadly for Hermia, he was within his right. For Athens' law allowed a father to choose his daughter's husband—or have her put to death if she refused. When Hermia announced she would rather die than marry a man she did not love, her father marched her off to the city's ruler to demand justice.

Soon to be married himself, Duke Theseus was sympathetic to Hermia's pleas of love. Yet the only other choice he could offer her was to enter a religious order and live in seclusion, never to see Lysander again.

"What shall we do?" wailed Hermia when she slipped away to meet her beloved for perhaps the very last time. "I cannot marry Demetrius. I love only you!"

"Dry your eyes, my sweet," said Lysander soothingly. "The course of true love never did run smooth. Besides—I have a plan."

"Tell me," said Hermia eagerly.

"I have an aunt who lives beyond Athens' borders. Tomorrow night slip from your father's house and meet me in the forest. We will flee to my aunt's home, and there be married free from Athens' law. If we—"

"Hush!" whispered Hermia. "Someone comes!"

She turned nervously, then smiled to see tall, willowy Helena. But her smile faded when she saw that her friend, usually so lovely, was pale and red-eyed from weeping over Demetrius.

"You look ill," said Hermia.

"Illness is catching," sniffed Helena. "If beauty were as well, I might catch yours, and in so doing win back the eye of Demetrius."

"Take comfort, dear friend," said Hermia. "Soon Demetrius shall no more see my face." Then, to ease Helena's sorrow, she revealed her plan to run away with Lysander. Alas, Helena was so ruled by the madness of love that she at once decided to tell the secret to Demetrius.

Surely he'll thank me for it, thought Helena, and in time perhaps return my love.

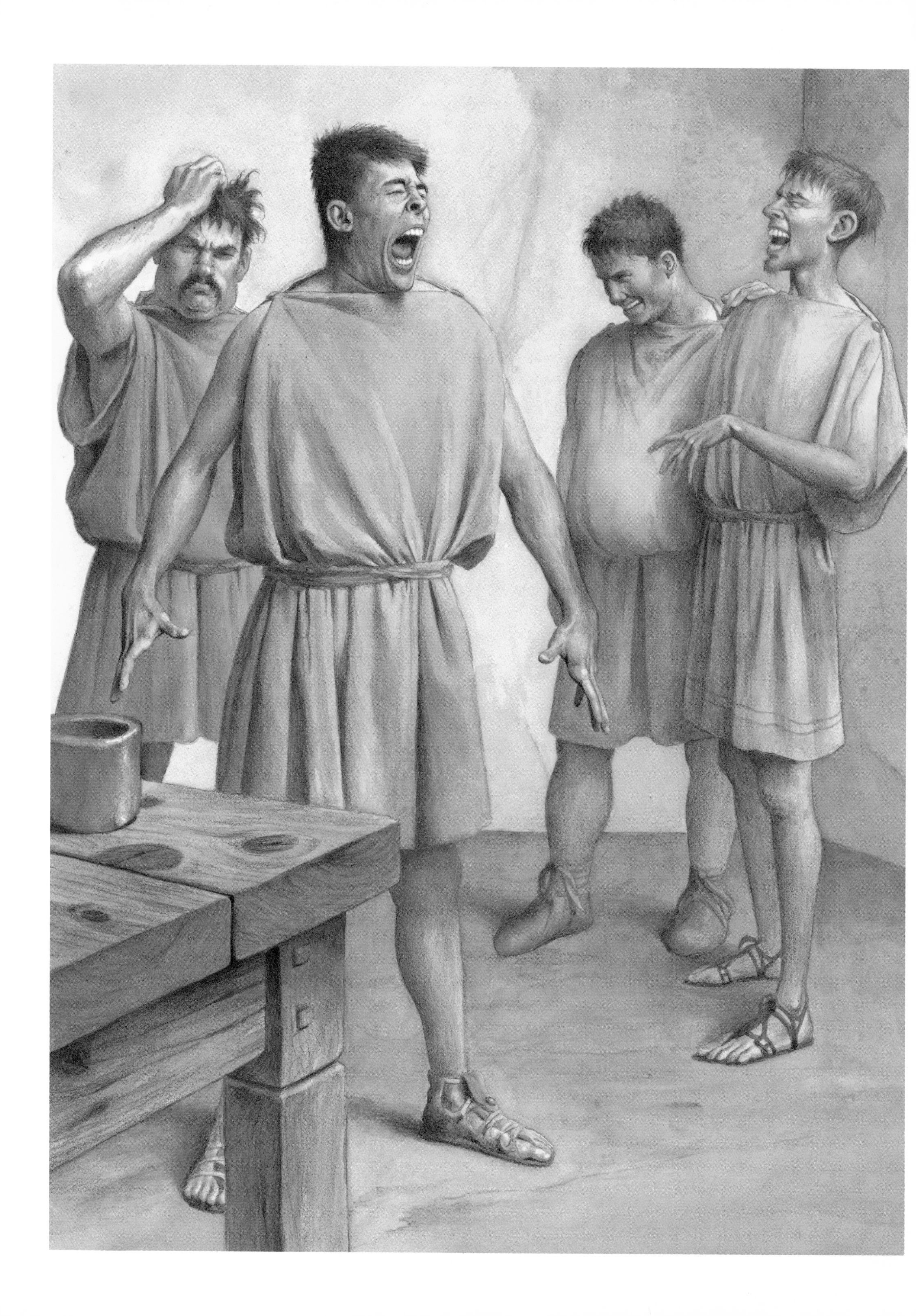

Elsewhere in the city a carpenter named Peter Quince had gathered his friends to put on a play in honor of the duke's wedding. He had chosen a weaver named Nick Bottom to play Pyramus, the hero.

"Is this Pyramus a lover, or a tyrant?" asked Bottom.

"A lover, who kills himself, most gallant, for love," replied Quince.

"Then the audience must mop their eyes," said Bottom happily. "For I shall make them weep like rainstorms. Even so, I would like to play a tyrant. I can rage like Hercules!" He began to demonstrate, howling and roaring until Quince begged him to stop so he could assign the rest of the parts.

The role of Thisby, the heroine, was given to young Francis Flute, the bellows mender. "Please, let me not be made to play a woman!" he cried. "I have a beard coming on."

"I'll play it!" said Bottom eagerly. "I'll wear a veil, and speak in a sweet, tiny voice."

"No, you must play Pyramus," said Quince firmly. "Now Snug, you shall be the lion."

"Let me, let me!" cried Bottom. "I shall roar and roar!"

"You will roar so much you frighten the ladies," said Quince. "Then we shall all be hanged."

"No hanging! No hanging!" cried the others, feeling their necks.

When Bottom was finally convinced to take only one role, Quince finished assigning parts. To rehearse in secret, the men agreed to meet the next night in the forest…the very forest where Hermia was to meet Lysander.

Before any human arrived the next night, the forest was already alive with bands of fairies and other strange creatures. One of these was a mischief-loving hobgoblin known as Puck.

"How now, spirit?" called Puck when he saw a fairy rushing by. "Whither do you wander?"

"Over hill and over dale, seeking dewdrops for Titania, the Fairy Queen," answered the tiny creature. "She will be here in but a moment."

Puck frowned. He knew his master Oberon, the Fairy King, would soon arrive as well. Oberon and Titania were locked in a bitter quarrel over a human child Titania had taken in when his mother died. Oberon wanted the boy to enter his service. But because the child's mother had been a devoted servant of Titania, the queen refused. Now whenever king and queen met, they did nothing but argue.

Before Puck could think of a way to prevent another fight, both Oberon and Titania entered the clearing.

"Ill met by moonlight, proud Titania," said Oberon.

The Fairy Queen curled her lip and turned to go.

"Wait!" called Oberon. "Why should Titania cross her Oberon? I ask but a mortal child to be my servant."

"I rear the boy for his mother's sake," replied Titania, "and for her sake I will not part with him. Oberon, do you not see how our quarrel has set the natural world in disorder? Fog and flood dismay the land. Crops rot in the field. The seasons themselves are in wild disorder. And all this flows from our dissent."

“Then grant me the boy and end this strife,” said Oberon.

“Not for all thy fairy kingdom,” snapped Titania. Waving her arms, she cried, “Fairies, away!” and she and all her company left the clearing.

When Titania was gone, Oberon turned to Puck and said, “In the far west grows a flower upon which Cupid once let his arrow fall. Now that flower’s juice, when squeezed upon sleeping eyelids, will make one fall madly in love with the first creature seen on waking. Fetch me that flower, sweet Puck.”

“I’ll put a girdle round about the earth in forty minutes,” said Puck, speeding from the clearing.

“This juice I’ll drop upon Titania’s eyes,” said Oberon to himself. “The next thing she sees upon waking, be it lion, bull, or busy ape, that will she pursue with all the soul of love. Nor will I use the antidote to remove the charm until the child is mine!”

Suddenly Oberon heard a man and a woman approaching, arguing loudly as they came. Fading into the shadows, he stayed to listen.

"Pursue me not!" cried Demetrius as he entered the clearing.

"You tell me not to pursue, yet you draw me like a magnet!" wept Helena, who was following him as closely as if they were head and tail of one animal.

"Have I not told you clearly that I do not love you?"

"That only makes me love you the more!"

"I am sick when I look on you!" roared Demetrius.

"And I am sick when I look not on you," moaned Helena. "I shall follow you as a dog follows its master."

"Have you no shame? No maiden modesty?" He looked around. "And where are Hermia and Lysander? You told me they would be here!" Muttering angrily, he stormed from the clearing to continue his search—with the lovesick Helena in pursuit.

Chuckling to himself, Oberon now saw another use for the flower he had sent Puck to fetch. When the sprite returned, the Fairy King said, "Take some of these blossoms. Search the wood till you find a weeping maid and the man who spurns her. You will know him by his clothing, which is that of an Athenian noble. Squeeze the juice upon the man's eyes when he sleeps. Meanwhile, I go to charm Titania."

The Fairy Queen had a flowery bank where she liked to rest. She was there now, assigning tasks to her tiny helpers, sending some to protect the rosebuds, others to battle bats for their wings, which made lovely coats for the tiniest elves. When this was done, she asked the remaining fairies to sing her to sleep, which they did in voices sweeter than any bird's. Thus did Oberon find his queen slumbering on a bed of wild thyme bowered over with musk roses and eglantine. Kneeling beside her, he squeezed the flower's juice upon her eyes and whispered, "That which you see when you awake, love and languish for its sake."

Meanwhile, Puck searched high and low for the Athenian noble he was to charm. He thought his quest ended when he came upon Lysander and Hermia. The lovers had lost their way in the wood and grown so weary of wandering, they had decided to rest. Because they were not yet married, Hermia had asked Lysander to lay a modest distance from her. When Puck saw the Athenian lying so far from the maiden, he was sure Lysander must be the one Oberon had sent him to enchant. Flitting down, the sprite squeezed the magical flower over Lysander's eyes.

Had Hermia been the first woman Lysander saw upon waking, all would have been well. But Helena too had lost her way and stumbled into the clearing. When she found Lysander flat upon the ground, she feared he was sick or wounded. "Lysander," she cried, shaking his shoulder. "Oh, Lysander, if you live, wake!"

Lysander opened his eyes, saw Helena, and was at once overtaken by the flower's magic. "For you, sweet Helena, I will not only wake, but run through fire!"

"Oh, my lord, do not say such things! What of your love for Hermia?"

"How can I love that raven, now that I see *you* clearly?"

Beaten down by Demetrius' scorn, Helena could not now believe any man loved her. She decided that Lysander must be making a cruel joke.

"I had thought you a lord of more true gentleness," she chided. "Must you mock the fact that no one loves me?" Then, with a whimper, she turned and fled into the woods.

Lysander, mad with the love spell, raced after her—leaving Hermia asleep and alone in the dark forest.

Meanwhile Quince, Bottom, and the others had gathered not far from Titania's bower to rehearse their play. Bottom was fretting over his part. "What if I am so convincing when I pretend to stab myself that I make the women faint? Surely then we will lose our heads."

Puck, who was on his way back to Oberon's side, overheard the players. "What hempen homespuns have we swaggering here?" he whispered. "More important—what fun can I have with them?"

Pondering merry mischief, the wicked sprite waited until the script called for Bottom to make an exit. Puck followed, and using his magic, gave Bottom the head of an ass.

Bottom did not notice the difference.

However, when he re-entered the clearing, his fellows screamed and fled, thinking him some terrible monster. "This is a joke of theirs to make me afraid," said Bottom. "Well, I'll not let them make an ass of me!" And he began to sing himself a song to keep up his courage.

His braying and bellowing woke Titania. The queen rose from her bed of flowers, saw the ass-headed monstrosity through magic-drenched eyes, and at once fell madly in love.

"I pray thee, gentle mortal," she called, "sing again. I do swear I love thee."

"Methinks, mistress, you should have little reason for that," said Bottom. "But then, reason and love keep little company these days."

"As wise as he is beautiful!" exclaimed Titania. "Come, I will give you fairies to attend you, to fetch you jewels from the deep, to sing you to sleep on beds of flowers." Then she called her four favorites—Peaseblossom, Cobweb, Moth, and Mustardseed—and told them to feed Bottom apricots and dewberries, and honey sacs snatched fresh from the bumblebee's belly.

Laughing merrily, Puck flew off to tell his lord what he had done.

"Better than I could have devised!" cried Oberon. "Now, here is what we must do next—"

But as Puck and Oberon began making plans, two humans entered the clearing.

"Stay," whispered Oberon. "Here is the young Athenian I told you of—the man, but not the woman!"

"It is the woman, but not the man!" replied Puck, puzzled.

Indeed, Hermia was now chasing Demetrius, whom she had stumbled upon while searching for her beloved Lysander. When she awoke to find him missing, she was sure that Demetrius was the cause of it. "Have you slain my love in his sleep?" she cried in a frenzy.

"Speak gently, dear one," pleaded Demetrius.

Hermia was in no mood for gentleness. "Coward! Will you not give me Lysander?"

"I'd sooner give his carcass to my hounds!" snapped Demetrius, losing his temper.

"Cur!" cried Hermia. "You drive me past the bounds of maiden's patience. Where is he that I love?"

"I do not know!"

"You do not know the truth, nor how to tell it! Since you will not help, I go to seek Lysander myself."

"You have charmed the wrong man!" whispered Oberon to Puck as Hermia ran into the darkness. "Quick! About the wood go swifter than the wind. Find tall, fair-haired Helena of Athens. Bring her here that we may set this right."

As the hobgoblin flitted off, Oberon laid a spell of weariness on Demetrius. At once the young man began to yawn. "There is no following Hermia when she is in this fierce mood," he muttered. "And I am exhausted. I must rest for a while."

Once he was sleeping soundly, Oberon bent and anointed his eyelids with the magical flower.

Puck returned soon after, luring with him not only Helena but Lysander, who still pursued her with cries of love.

"Lord, what fools these mortals be!" chortled Puck. He could hardly wait for the scene that would follow when the magic worked again, and both Demetrius and Lysander were vying for Helena's hand.

The sprite did not have to wait long. Lysander was shouting loud enough to wake every spirit of the forest. "Forget Demetrius!" he roared. "He loves Hermia, not you!"

This roused Demetrius, who opened his eyes, saw Helena, and cried, "Goddess! Nymph! Oh, soul of perfection, let me but kiss your hand and bliss is mine!"

Helena turned to him in a rage. "Are you in on the joke as well? What a pair of men you are, mocking this poor maiden."

"No mockery," protested Lysander, "but love most true. It is Demetrius who toys with you. If he will give up his false claim of love, I will gladly give him Hermia."

Before the argument could go any further, Hermia burst into the clearing. "There you are, my love!" she cried, throwing her arms about Lysander. "Why did you leave me alone in this dark wood?"

"Why should I stay, when love for fair Helena did press me to go?" he asked, trying to pry himself from her embrace.

"What!" gasped Hermia in horror. "This cannot be!"

"Look how she pretends!" said Helena. "She too is part of this cruel jest! Ungrateful friend to join such men. After all we two have shared, how can you scorn me so?"

"I scorn you not!" cried Hermia.

"Did you not set these men who worship you to pursue me with words of false love?"

"Not false, but truest of true," moaned Demetrius.

"Yet not half so true as the love I offer," said Lysander.

Hermia turned to Helena and shrieked, "You thief of love! Did you come by night and steal my love's heart? Did you turn Lysander's head because you are so tall and I so short? I am not so low my nails cannot reach your eyes, you painted maypole!"

"I pray you, gentlemen, though you mock me, let her not hurt me!" wept Helena.

"Get you gone, you dwarf," said Lysander to Hermia.

"Speak not so swiftly on Helena's part," interrupted Demetrius. "She is *my* love, and *I* will defend her."

"Defend yourself!" challenged Lysander. "Follow me, if you dare fight for love."

As the two men left the clearing to do battle, Oberon whispered to Puck, "This is all your fault!"

"I did no more than you asked, King of Shadows," the sprite replied. "I squeezed the flower over the eyes of a young man wearing the clothes of Athens. Besides, what sorrow in my error? Is this not fine sport?"

"They seek a place to fight," said Oberon. "Hurry, overcast the night with drooping fog. Mimicking each man's voice, lead them away from each other. Goad them to strike out at the empty air until they are exhausted. Here is the antidote to our charm. After you have worn Lysander to a sleep, drop some on his eyelids. When he wakes, his affections shall turn right, and all this quarrel seem but a dream."

As Puck sped off to untangle the lovers' woes, Oberon made his way to Titania's bower. He found his queen fondling Bottom's long ears, while the four tiny fairies wound flowers in his hair and scratched his chin.

"What delicacy would please your tongue?" asked Titania.

"Actually, I'd like a bale of hay," replied Bottom.

"What is this I see?" roared Oberon, coming upon them as if he were surprised. He began to chide Titania for her strange love, until she was so shamed she agreed to give Oberon the serving boy. The king accepted and left her side—but only to hide behind a tree and cast the spell of sleep. Then he called Puck to his side.

In a trice the sprite was there.

"Is it done?" asked Oberon.

"I have drawn them all together, and left them sound asleep," said Puck.

The king smiled. "And I have gained the boy. Now that I have him, I will remove the spell from Titania's eyes. Meanwhile, you remove the ass's head from this Athenian, so that when he wakes, he, like the others, will think all was but a dream."

When the sun's rays began to kiss the treetops, Duke Theseus led his bridal party to the forest to perform some important wedding rituals. The group was astonished to find the four young people, who were just waking from their strange night.

Hermia's father, who accompanied the duke, swelled with rage when he learned that Hermia and Lysander had run away to elope. But Demetrius announced that he now loved only Helena, so the old man was left sputtering.

The two happy couples headed back to Athens trying to untangle the threads of the previous night. But not one could say what was a dream, and what was real.

Bottom was the last to wake. "I have had a most rare vision," he said. "A dream to pass the wit of man to say what dream it was." With a headful of strange memories, he made his way back to the city, still hoping to join his friends in presenting their play at Theseus' wedding.

That night, after the wedding not only of Theseus but of the two young couples as well, the duke's new bride said, "'Tis passing strange, the tale these lovers tell."

"More strange than true," replied the duke, shaking his head. "Lovers and madmen have such seething brains. But look, here come the young lovers now. Joy, gentle friends! Joy and fresh days of love accompany your hearts!"

Then he called for entertainment to cap the evening and—of all the choices offered by his master of revels—picked Quince's tale of Pyramus and Thisby.

Quince began by introducing the players. One, carrying a lantern and leading a dog, portrayed the man in the moon. Poor Francis Flute with his new beard coming in had been stuffed into a dress to play Thisby. But of course Bottom received the lion's share of the attention, ending the play with the most absurd death scene anyone had ever witnessed.

So the players needn't have worried about losing their heads: Their version of the terrible tragedy was so ridiculous that the audience nearly burst with laughter.

Play ended, players and audience alike drifted off to bed. Then Oberon and Titania flew into the palace, bringing with them bands of fairies who scattered through the halls to drop their blessings on all who slept in true love's dreamy thrall.

A NOTE FROM THE AUTHOR

In the introduction to her book of retellings of Shakespeare, the great E. Nesbit mentions taking her daughters to visit the playwright's house. Inspired by their trip, and their mother's enthusiasm, the girls attempted to read *A Midsummer Night's Dream*. Not surprisingly, it didn't take long before one of them sighed and said, "I can't understand a word of it!"

Finally they prevailed upon their mother to simply tell them the story. When she did, they were enchanted.

"Why don't you write the stories for us so that we can understand them," suggested Iris. "Then, when we are grown up, we shall understand the plays so much better!"

It was a good idea then, and possibly an even better one now, when young readers need even more help and encouragement to find their way to the treasure trove awaiting them in Shakespeare's work. Early exposure to a tale as delightful as *A Midsummer Night's Dream* can do much to defuse the fear of Shakespeare that is an unfortunate side effect of the poet's towering reputation. And who is not richer for having met Bottom, Puck, Titania, and Oberon early in life? Indeed, knowing such characters is an essential part of what we have come to call "cultural literacy."

The greatest difficulty facing anyone attempting a faithful adaptation of this particular story comes with the romantic leads, for as Shakespearean scholar Catherine Belsey says, "The four lovers are virtually indistinguishable." This hardly represents sloppy writing on Shakespeare's part; rather it is his commentary on the arbitrary nature of romantic love.

Fortunately, in the same way that actors can make it easier for the audience to keep track of these ciphers, having an illustrated version helps readers to follow their adventures.

The major cut I made in the retelling was to trim the relative weight given to the last act, which consists largely of Quince and company's play-within-a-play. While on stage this can give rise to inspired buffoonery, it does not add to the plot so much as comment on it.

Finally, this book is not meant to be a substitute for Shakespeare's original play, but a gateway to the greater enjoyment of it, whether on the page or on the stage.

HERMIA
LYSANDER
DEMETRIUS
HELENA